6-in-1

Aesop's Fables

Stories by Ken Spillman

Art by Suvidha Mistry

SCHOLASTIC
New York Toronto London Auckland
Sydney New Delhi Hong Kong

Published by Scholastic India Pvt. Ltd.
A subsidiary of Scholastic Inc., New York, 10012 (USA).
Publishers since 1920, with international operations in Canada, Australia, New Zealand, the United Kingdom, India, and Hong Kong.

For information regarding permission, write to:
Scholastic India Pvt. Ltd.
A-27, Ground Floor, Sigma Centre
Infocity-1, Sector 34, Gurgaon 122001 (India)

ISBN-13: 978-93-5275-634-6

First edition: November 2018

This reprint edition, April 2025

Printed at Acme Print O Pac Pvt. Ltd. Noida

Introduction

Do you know that a person who writes fables is called a fabulist?

And that fables rank high among the most enduring stories of all time?

The fables of Aesop and the Panchatantra were both written more than 2,000 years ago, yet are still read by millions. The world may have changed, but we still find wisdom in these fine feats of fabulist imagination.

Why? Because a fable conveys a moral that can help us understand ourselves, as well as the people we encounter as we live our lives. Morals are better than even the most useful gadgets. Once absorbed, they are not only portable but invisible. Most don't go out of style and are guaranteed to last forever. How cool is that?

According to legend—and legends are legendary for being true, right?—Aesop was a far-from-handsome slave in ancient Greece. He gained his freedom by being clever!

Reading these stories inspired by Aesop's fabulous fables will not make you ugly, but it will certainly help make you clever.

Have some fun, readers!

Ken Spillman

Contents

The Frogs and their King

"We are all born equal," announced a big green frog to his peers. "That is the beauty of being amphibian."

He was holding forth on a lily pad and looked rather grand, his patterned skin glistening in the last of the day's sun. Although he wasn't quite the largest of the frogs in the pond, he had developed a habit of speaking with authority, puffing himself up with words.

"The beauty of being amphibian indeed!" his lady friend scoffed. "Only a frog would say that. Correction, only *you* would say something like that."

Around the pond, other frogs could be seen clinging to

reeds, perched on sticks or squatting on lily pads like the pair in conversation. A few were listening, though most were not. Among their number were many who rarely spoke a word, regarding words as indulgences in a world where it was far more important to keep watch for birds and snakes and tasty little flies. There were tadpoles to watch over, too—though it was well-nigh impossible to keep track of whose babies were whose.

"Big fellow," called a cheeky young frog who liked nothing better than challenging his elders. "You seem to think that equality is a blessing." This frog had decided while still a tadpole that he was brilliant—much too brilliant to be anybody's equal.

"Of course it is," replied the bigger of the two in his deep, gruff voice. "Don't you?"

"Well, perhaps you don't possess the vision to see how things might be better if they were different." Though the cheeky frog had never really considered this himself until now, he let his sentence hang in the air as if he had pondered it through many a long day.

"He's quite right," said the large frog's lady friend. "We should never simply assume that the way things *are* is exactly how they *should be*."

The large frog didn't seem to appreciate this contribution and shot her a disgruntled glance. He rearranged his toes on the lily pad before addressing his chief source of irritation directly.

"Tell me, then, if you must, how things might be better—in your own humble opinion, of course."

The younger frog had by now hit upon an idea which, like all his ideas, he felt sure was clever enough to announce to the world. He hadn't held the idea long enough in his head to actually *believe* in his clever words but, truth be told, *sounding* clever had always been more important to him than *being* clever.

"There is nothing wrong with equality," he began, "as long as there is leadership." Suddenly he noticed that almost all of the frogs around the pond had turned their heads to listen. This emboldened him further, and he projected his voice across the still water as if rallying imaginary troops.

"Our progress as a community depends on that and that alone, leadership. Unfortunately, we cling blindly to the belief that we frogs are all equal, which only means that we pay no heed to merit. In this pond, the best and brightest carry no sway over the dopy and dull-witted."

At this, many in his audience croaked and chirruped. Every frog, regardless of age or gender, felt certain that a list of the pond's best and brightest was bound to include them.

"What we need is a supreme being, a ruler who stands apart from us and quite above us. Under the sovereignty of a ruler, our pond would not be so, well ..." He waved a front leg around, searching for the right word. "Our pond would not be so ... *stagnant.*"

A couple of frogs gasped. Many nodded to each other. The large, proud frog gave out a low croak of displeasure.

"Hold your tongue, dear," urged his wife. "No need to turn this into an argument."

The younger frog was so very satisfied with his choice of word that he wanted immediately to repeat it. "Yes, friends, we are stagnant. Equality is pleasant, in its way, but who do we have to look up to? Without a ruler we have no direction."

The older frog could take this no more. "If you are so keen to be ruled, and to have the direction of a sovereign, why don't you see if the gods will oblige?"

"Very well," responded the cocky young frog. "As long as you remember that the gods do not *always* choose to make things easy for us. Whether they act in our interests is a matter for their wisdom."

"Of course," came the reply. "There is nothing more self-evident than that."

At that, the young frog called for a mighty chorus from all those who saw the good sense in asking the gods for a ruler. Together they raised their voices to the heavens, beseeching the gods to deliver them a monarch.

No sooner had they done so than a huge log splashed into the pond. It sent water flying and probably cost the lives of any number of poor tadpoles. Frogs darted away, terrified. For quite some time there was an awed silence.

"Long live the King," came the voice of the young frog who had led the chorus of prayer.

"Oh great and powerful King, we welcome you and thank the gods who sent you," said another.

Many other frogs called out to proclaim their loyalty, and even the large frog whose words had resulted in this astonishing event felt moved to speak.

His low, rumbling croak rang out across the pond. "As your subjects, good King, we are equals, and equally subject to your command."

The log, however, commanded nothing. The frogs suspected that the effort of falling and making such a gigantic splash might have exhausted him. They decided to let him rest.

Come the next day, however, the King was still at rest.

Come the next week, the unbroken rest of the monarch was beginning to cause *un*rest among the frogs.

"What kind of King is this?" one frog asked.

"Quite a wooden one," quipped another.

The large, green, outspoken frog had an idea. "Perhaps, my friends, our King has detected the perfection of our society and sees no reason for royal intervention. He wishes to be no more than a figurehead."

"Nonsense," laughed his lady friend. "Figurehead! Even a figurehead can listen, and this log is as deaf as a post. He's lazy, that's all. Can't even be bothered telling us his name."

"Maybe he's King Lazy the Third?" suggested a comedian in the group.

"What happened to the first two King Lazys?"

"In all probability, they are flat out ruling other ponds."

Even the young frog who had led the community in calling for a ruler laughed at this. He was bitterly disappointed with the gods and could not accept their choice of a king for his pond. They had embarrassed him and, though he knew it would seem ungrateful to beseech the gods again, saw no alternative. One morning, he attracted the attention of all the other frogs with a loud succession of high-pitched cawing sounds.

"With due respect to our beloved King, I think we would agree that his reign has not been all we hoped it might be." The young frog paused for a moment, appreciating the silent consent of his audience. "Monarchies thrive on timely succession. Perhaps now is the time for the gods to name a successor."

"This King is fine," croaked the large frog. "He lets us *be*—what more could we ask for?"

The young frog was not to be deterred. "He lets us be, that is true. He lets us be *mediocre*."

"Speak for yourself," the large frog croaked back.

The old fellow received a sharp kick from the powerful hind leg of his lady friend. "No need to be rude," she said.

Some frogs were nervous that the gods may be displeased if they were called upon to name another ruler for the pond

so soon. Yet the fact that the gods had obliged them once encouraged a belief that they might do so again, perhaps more satisfactorily.

The frogs raised their voices to the heavens once more. They cried out for leadership, for an active ruler who would truly stand above them, making waves and changing their pond world forever.

The gods were more than displeased about being pestered in this way, and cast down their wrath in the form of a heron.

Silence fell. The heron strutted along the log it had succeeded as ruler and the frogs bowed down before their new King.

"Sire, I am at your service," announced the cheeky young frog, keen to make a good first impression. "I welcome having someone I can truly look up to."

The heron leaned over, took him in its beak and swallowed the frog before he could utter another word.

"Already things are looking up under this King's reign," said the older frog—but then *he* was eaten too.

The heron was soon making a great feast of his subjects, and many frogs, wondering if service to the King should really include satisfying his appetite, hopped for their lives.

This was to no avail. They were all, in the eyes of their King, equally tasty and they were also equal in death.

The Miser

There was once a merchant who hated nothing more than spending money.

"That miser will be the death of me," his wife told anyone who would listen. "As night follows day, he will grumble about the cost of my funeral."

Those words were prophetic, for she indeed grew old before her time, worn out by the effort of nagging and pleading with her husband for the trappings of a life worthy of their class. When she died, the merchant complained bitterly.

"Expensive in life and just as expensive in death," he told his brother. "I thank god that she did not bear any children."

By means of the woman's persistence, however, the couple had gradually accumulated many fineries.

She had purchased jewellery and silk so that she could socialise with other merchants' wives without feeling like a poor village girl. She had bought glassware and bone china so that they might host dinners for visiting traders. She had filled their house with ornaments and art.

With the extreme care she had been forced to exercise in her spending, the woman had always sought expert advice. As a result, much of what she bought had increased enormously in value over the years of their marriage.

The merchant himself, however, attached little value to any of these possessions. He had spent a lifetime trading goods for gold, and he soon decided that this was exactly what he would do with all that he now owned.

He sold his wife's jewellery and the art that hung on the walls of his house. He sold furniture, china, even books. Finally he sold the house itself, buying instead a tiny cabin on the edge of town. With all his cash, he purchased an ingot of solid gold.

The merchant loved that gold more than he had ever loved anything—including his long-suffering wife.

"Now," he thought to himself, "how can I keep my gold safe?"

He disliked banks, since they only made money from other people's hard work and good fortune. If he lodged his gold at a bank, they would charge for its safekeeping and he would only be able to see his gold during business hours.

For this reason, the merchant decided to hide his gold in a secret location not far from his little cabin.

One night, under the cover of darkness, he dug a hole beside an old stone wall. He lined it with fleece, placed the ingot inside and covered it in such a way that passers-by would never detect what lay below the surface.

It happened, however, that a farm labourer in a nearby field observed a number of the man's visits to the spot. Intrigued, he waited for an opportunity to investigate.

Upon exposing the hole, the labourer could not believe his

eyes. The riches it contained were far beyond anything he had ever imagined—but they were not beyond his capacity to remove. He promptly did so and was never seen in the region again.

When the merchant discovered the theft, he started tearing at his hair. He wailed so loud, and for so long, that many presumed that his wife's death had belatedly struck at his emotions. His wife's family, still in mourning, sent the man's brother-in-law to console him. Grief shared, they thought, would aid in his recovery.

The brother-in-law fumed silently as the merchant told him of the only loss that had ever caused him pain—the gold he had loved and hidden in vain.

Finally, the brother-in-law could contain himself no longer.

"My family grieves for the woman who was your faithful wife," he began. "*Your* suffering, on the other hand, is attached to an object. It has neither lived nor died. I say to you—take a stone, place it in that hiding place of yours, and convince yourself it is gold."

"What value has a stone?" countered the merchant.

"Your gold has no more value than a stone, if you make not the slightest use of it."

With that, the brother-in-law rose from his chair. He left the merchant's cabin and never spoke to the miser again.

The Fox and the Goat

A fox is as proud as it is cunning—and pride, when extreme, can lead to a fall. Few foxes are so careless as to fall into a well, but such peculiar events are not unheard of.

One young fox, light on his feet and possessing fine balance, wanted more than anything to see himself in motion.

"What a glorious sight that must be," he told other foxes. "It is so terribly unfair that you can freely witness my grace—but that I, myself, cannot!"

Other foxes believed there was little point telling this fellow that he moved in a manner typical of their species, and that he could get the general idea by watching any one of them.

Consequently, the fox himself devised a plan. He would go to a nearby well and leap across it, watching his reflection in the water as he did so. It was this hare-brained scheme that led to the accident.

On the fox's fifth jump, he tried to reproduce the action of running while still in the air. Intent on catching a glimpse of this in the mirror below, he misjudged his landing and tumbled rather ungracefully into the well.

The fox was fortunate. The water was deep enough to cushion his landing—yet wasn't too deep for him to stand in. He felt foolish, and hoped no other fox had witnessed the incident. At that moment, his greatest fear was that he would become a laughing stock.

Then, far greater fears seized him. His mind raced as he considered his plight.

How will I get out of here? Even if another fox witnessed my fall, what could it do? Our kind is not known for its expertise with ropes and pulleys.

I cannot jump high enough to reach the top—not even if I had the advantage of a good run-up.

These walls are impossible for me to climb. Might I starve?

There and then, the fox realised that he needed to make full use of his intelligence. Whereas previously he had exercised little care and even less brainpower, these and these alone could now save him. And if he should survive, he decided, he would never forget his lesson.

A day passed and, try as he might, the fox was unable to conceive a plan that would save him. Cold and hungry though he was, however, he did not give up.

Finally, he heard the rasping voice of a goat from above.

"Good fellow," the goat said. "I'm dreadfully thirsty. How is the water?"

The fox thought quickly.

"Clean and refreshing! Come in, come in! Perhaps this water even has some magical property, for it has given me wisdom. I was once an old and mangy fox, would you believe? Now look at my coat—a little wet, but *magnificent.* I feel young again, young enough to ..."

Before the fox could conclude his attractive advertisement of the well, the goat jumped in beside him. The parched goat drank as if the water might evaporate if he paused for even an instant.

The fox was pleased with this turn of events. He watched the goat with satisfaction.

"You see? You may never feel thirsty again."

The goat could only nod a little as he drank.

Eventually, however, he lifted his head and gave out a loud sigh of contentment. "Thank you, sir. I needed that!" Then the goat looked up. "Now, what is the best way to get out?"

"That is a matter I have considered most carefully," said the fox. He spoke with authority—for, indeed, a plan had been forming in his mind since the first appearance of the

goat. "First, you will help me by acting as a stepladder. Once I am out, I will pull you up to the top."

To the goat, this sounded reasonable. He stood on his hind legs and rested his front hooves against the wall. The fox scrambled up the gullible goat's shoulders and steadied himself before, with one mighty effort, leaping out of the well.

He turned to the goat. "Farewell, my friend, and thank you for your assistance."

"You cannot leave!" the goat protested. "We had a plan. You must now help me!"

"Even if I should have the brute strength and the implements required to hoist you out, I would think twice," the fox gloated. "After all, I found myself in the well by accident but you dived in like a fool. Had you examined the situation, you might have seen the need for an exit plan. You exposed yourself to dangers from which you had no means of escape."

With that, the fox shook water from his coat and set off in the direction of a henhouse. The sun and freedom warmed him to the core.

The Hare and the Tortoise

There was once a young hare who took great pleasure in bragging, and ragging his friends. Naturally, other hares soon started avoiding him. The hare, supposing there was no better way of passing his days, then directed his boastfulness at other poor animals.

One day, the hare spied an old tortoise making her way along a well-worn track.

"Aha! She looks like fair game!"

He bounded up to the tortoise as if he had to announce something of great importance. The tortoise knew the hare's reputation and tried ignoring him.

"What a slow old thing you are," started the hare. The tortoise kept up her steady, plodding pace, saying nothing.

"If not for your beady eyes," the hare continued, "I'd have mistaken you for a rock."

Again, the tortoise held her silence.

"Oh, now I see," said the hare, "you actually do have legs! Goodness! Look at the way they move—like clouds when there's only the tiniest puff of breeze. So cute!"

The old tortoise had been called many things in her long life, but 'cute' wasn't one of them. The hare's scorn was just too much.

"What's a hare anyway?" she asked. "A lanky rabbit with outsized ears? A bunny that lost the creation lottery?"

The hare opened his mouth in mock surprise. "She speaks!"

The tortoise kept walking, her shell swaying and listing as she went. While there was no hope of peace now, she could at least continue on her way.

"If I were as slow as you, I wouldn't bother moving at all," the hare said. "I'd forget where I was going long before I ever arrived anywhere ..."

Now, the tortoise stopped. "Don't you realise that haste is one of the world's greatest problems? You and your like go from point A to point B without ever noticing how you got there. It's a crying shame, it really is!"

"Better than never getting there," snapped the hare in reply.

The tortoise could see that her words had pricked the young fellow's nerves. "Don't you worry," she told him. "I do get to every place I set out for. In just the right time, if you ask me. Yes, you run like the wind. I'm more attached to the earth. But, if it appeals to you, I will race you anytime you choose."

The hare threw his head back and laughed, his ears flopping every which way.

"Are you up to the challenge—or not?" the tortoise asked. She knew that she had nothing to lose. "If yes, we must find a referee and have the course set for us."

The hare finally seemed at a loss for words. To such a haughty fellow, the idea of taking the tortoise's proposal seriously seemed ridiculous. Yet, he could not afford to dismiss it. Doing so would mean surrendering the upper hand in their exchange.

"Very well," the hare said finally. "Let Mr Fox set the course. He can applaud me at the finishing line—just don't expect us to wait for you to finish as well."

Off went the hare in search of Mr Fox. The tortoise rested under a tree, somewhat surprised by the day's turn of events, awaiting its next chapter.

Mr Fox was a distinguished chap, as grey as any fox can be. At some point in life, he had adopted an air of boredom, and the planned race had aroused little interest in him. It was, he said, a chore he could live without. Nevertheless, the hare was a pest to be reckoned with, and he pestered Mr Fox until he agreed.

When the tortoise saw the hare returning with their referee, she knew that the race she had so whimsically suggested was just minutes away.

"The things we mortals do!" said Mr Fox, with a gaping yawn. "Can't you two think of a more amusing way of wasting time?" He looked at the tortoise disdainfully. "At your age, madam, you should be above such follies."

"You have been asked to referee a race, not judge my character," replied the tortoise.

"Oh, you're as tiresome as he is," Mr Fox said. "But let's get this over and done with."

Mr Fox carefully described a path that would take the pair past the first three landmarks he could think of. They would return to the tree under which they all stood. He drew a line in the sand and waited as the contestants took their place behind it.

"On your marks, get set ..." The hare coiled himself up like a spring. The tortoise scarcely moved, and Mr Fox eyed her suspiciously. "Madam, are you quite sure you're ready? You look far from it, if you ask me."

"Fear not, I am poised to blast off and zoom into the distance as only a tortoise can," she replied rather tartly.

"Get set ... GO!"

The hare disappeared in a blur of motion and a cloud of dust. The tortoise coughed a little and put her best foot forward. This caused a second foot, diagonally opposite, to budge as well. Then she thrust her next best foot forward. She was off and racing!

"Oh dear," said Mr Fox, shaking his head. "I really should have brought something to pass the time."

When the hare reached a large rock, the first landmark Mr Fox had nominated, he looked back. His ears swivelled back and forth. Unable to see or hear the tortoise at all, he sniffed the air. There was no scent of her either. Instead, the hare picked up the unmistakable aroma of ... mmm ... fresh, ripe apples, fallen from a tree. The hare followed his nose.

"No harm in a snack," he said grandly, though only the rock was listening.

Meanwhile, the tortoise found herself regretting her race idea. "Oh well," she thought, "if this takes me all day, I must stay the course—or lose my pride."

She plodded on, settling into a rhythm that went:

One, nearly two, two ...

Three, nearly four, four.

She observed clusters of flowers as she went. She watched the play of shadows around her and listened to birdsong. But not once did she break her stride.

The hare was now pausing at the second landmark, a goat crossing. His snack had become a meal, and he was feeling quite full. This had slowed his progress a little, but the tortoise was still nowhere to be seen or even heard. He could win by an hour, or by many hours—what was the difference? Mr Fox was unlikely to wait for both of them to finish, so the margin of the hare's victory would probably be his own to concoct.

At the final landmark, where a bubbling brook flowed into a pond, the hare did not look into the distance for the tortoise. Neither did he listen for her, or test the air for her scent. She was, he knew, far away.

The hare drank from the pond and nestled into the soft grass at the base of a tree. "Ah, this is the life," he said. Realising that he was his only listener, he added, "Yes, indeed it is!"

The scene was tranquil and the sound of flowing water replaced the voice of conceit. A stomach full of apples brews deep contentment and, when sleep fell upon the hare, it wasn't a light snooze. The hare drifted deep into the world of dreams.

When eventually the tortoise reached the brook, she could hardly believe her eyes. She considered waking her young rival to remind him that he was supposed to be contesting a race—but then dismissed the thought as quickly as the hare had left her in a swirl of dust at the starting line.

"He'll wake soon, no doubt," she thought. "And if he doesn't, it will teach him a lesson."

On she went:

One, nearly two, two ...

Three, nearly four, four.

Mr Fox too had been napping. Before drifting off, he had cursed himself again for agreeing to such an absurdity. A race between a young hare and an old tortoise? Could anything be less suspenseful? What nonsense!

When the hare woke from his slumber, he was uncertain how long he had slept. The shadows around the pond, however, were longer than they had been when he arrived, and the sun was lower in the sky. He shook himself and raced on.

Drawing within sight of the finishing line, the hare looked for Mr Fox and saw him curled up in the shade. "Goodness," thought the hare, "the old fox waited!" Then, to his horror, he spotted the old tortoise. She was ahead of him, closing in on victory. How could it be!

The hare dashed for the line, covering the ground even faster than he had when the race had begun. It was to no avail. The tortoise crossed first and had time to wake Mr Fox

so that he could watch the hare finish the race in the position he had not, until then, contemplated.

Second.

"I may be slow," the tortoise told the hare, "but I am also ..."

"Steady," Mr Fox chimed in. He was, for once, entertained. "Steady is what she is. And steady madam will always be." He winked at the hare. "Maybe that is what counts, young fellow!"

The Trees and the Axe

A woodcutter without a fine axe is like a baker without an oven. He can think of nothing except finding a remedy for the situation, for an axe is his meal ticket, the blade with which he might fashion his dreams. But an axe without its handle is worthless, a promise that cannot be kept.

Long ago, there was a strapping woodcutter with a growing family to feed. He worked so long and at such a furious pace that, by day's end, he had barely enough energy to sharpen the blade of his axe. Its handle was neglected. It became dry, chipped and fragile. Eventually, it snapped.

Demand for the woodcutter's wood was high. With winter approaching, his neighbours were hoarding firewood, repairing cottages and completing new barns. If he could not cut timber and split logs today, there would be nothing to sell to them tomorrow.

Loath to spend three days and three nights travelling to the nearest market, he considered his options. Axe handles used by professionals need special qualities—they should not just have above average strength but excellent flexibility to increase durability and soften the impact

absorbed by the arms. The woodcutter knew that the wood of the ash tree was ideal.

He set out for a nearby forest. This was a place of unsurpassed beauty. It had stood against the spread of farms, and had, through some unwritten covenant, been spared the blows of timber men. It provided refuge for animals and birds not seen elsewhere.

Upon the woodcutter's arrival, he stood in awe of the forest's scale and grandeur. Then, without forethought, he began to speak. His voice was loud, as if calling from a hilltop across a valley.

"O forest," he declaimed, "I come with a request. I am a poor woodcutter. I supply wood to those who need shelter and warmth. Give me one small ash sapling from your abundance, that it may be shaped and fitted as my axe handle."

Immediately, the most imposing of the trees could be heard whispering. The woodcutter ventured into the forest and found an ash sapling that would serve his purpose. He looked up and listened.

From the great height of the old trees, the sapling the man had chosen seemed tiny. It had seen few winters and

was barely old enough to withstand a forest fire. No bird had yet seen fit to nest in it.

"This is a modest request," the trees decided. Their verdict was in favour of the man, even as the ash before him cried out.

After felling the ash with his hatchet, the man returned home. Using a chisel and a knife, he began whittling the wood according to his needs. As he did so, he began to feel greater than he was, empowered by the forest and its indulgence in an unexpected way. It was as if the forest had now joined him in his enterprise.

The next day, and for many days thereafter, the man returned to the forest to cut timber, chopping down even some of the most noble giants. No longer did he stand in awe of the forest. The forest stood in terror of him.

An old oak tree, lamenting the loss of so many of its companions, swayed and sighed in the cold autumn wind.

"Alas, alas! We have only ourselves to blame. The little we gave cost us dearly. If we had not been so careless in casting aside the rights of that poor ash, we might have retained our privileges and stood in sanctuary forever."

The Salt Merchant's Donkey

Salt has always had value, for the smallest taste of it is an enticement to take more than is needed. In bulk, of course, salt is heavy, so the first priority of a salt merchant is to establish a reliable means of carriage.

Stories are told of a salt merchant whose sturdy young donkey was generously treated. The merchant was aware of its value to his livelihood. Together they plied a trade between the seaside and a wide circuit of villages. They climbed hills, wended their way through forests, and crossed plains. To the merchant, the donkey seemed a willing worker. Whenever it got tired, he let it rest. And whenever it stumbled, he spoke kindly to it, without any rebuke.

One day, they were crossing a stream after taking on a full load of salt by the sea. The donkey stumbled on the bed of round, slippery pebbles and completely lost its footing. Such an accident had never occurred before, and the animal felt a sharp jab to its pride. When the donkey struggled to its feet, however,

it was surprised to find that the load in its salt panniers was much lighter.

Since the donkey hardly knew about salt's ability to dissolve in water, it was delighted.

"How astonishing!" it mused. "Water not only refreshes, but also works its magic on dead weight! If I remember this, my work will be easier. My master will be pleased, for unloading quickly means we can take more load."

The salt merchant, of course, was not as pleased as the donkey fancied. Indeed, it was he who now felt a heavy load upon his shoulders. Watching his freight ruined in such a way was like seeing gold become bricks—except that the merchant didn't even have bricks to sell.

Nevertheless, the man kept his despair to himself. "Accidents happen," he said. "That is life. To take my disappointment out on the poor donkey would serve no purpose at all."

He bathed in the stream—which, despite all the salt that had disappeared into it, still tasted as fresh as the water at its source. Then he turned the donkey back in the direction of the sea.

They reached their destination and refilled the panniers with salt. After taking some refreshment and rest, they set out again.

As the merchant approached the stream where the accident had happened, he saw that the donkey was becoming agitated. It tossed its head and snorted.

"It's not like you to be nervy," the merchant told the donkey. "You have only slipped once so far, so the chances of slipping a second time are trifling."

The animal, meanwhile, was thinking only of magic.

Crossing the stream, the donkey plunged to its knees and felt the cool water flow around its body. It had emptied the panniers without the merchant lifting a finger.

It brayed triumphantly.

The merchant was furious. He had driven donkeys for long enough to be able to distinguish an accident from a swim, and could see that this was no accident. He feared that he had lost more than a load of salt—he had probably lost a donkey. In business, an animal that cannot be relied upon is worse than no animal at all.

Tethering the donkey to a tree, he sat by the water for a very long time.

The donkey, meanwhile, was perplexed. The magic had worked again, yet the man was clearly displeased.

"Human beings are such strange creatures," the donkey thought. "They give us heavy loads, yet seem happy when, little by little, they manage to reduce that very same load. All I have done is hasten this process for my master. He didn't complain before—why isn't he celebrating now?"

The salt merchant devised, in the depths of his despair, a possible solution. He reasoned that the donkey lacked the capacity to fully understand the consequences of its actions, otherwise, why would it risk being traded to a cruel owner, or being sold for its hide? By chance, the donkey had learned a clever trick. In its simplicity, it had tried it again. He mused, "Now, how can I teach this beast that its trick is not so clever after all?"

Upon his return to the sea, the merchant filled the panniers with sponges. He purchased a small fishing net, which he also filled with sponges, and strapped it across the donkey's hindquarters. He then set out for the stream.

The donkey believed that its fortuitous discovery of water magic was now being rewarded. Finally, its master was favouring lighter loads. It was wonderful!

Arriving at the stream, the merchant again sensed the excitement of his beast, and again tried to reassure him.

"Once was bad luck. Twice was carelessness. I hope and trust you will not be so reckless again."

But, light though the sponges were, the donkey thought they might just as well become lighter. Midstream, it fell to its knees again. When the donkey attempted to stand, it could

not. The sponges were soaked to capacity, and lifting them all would have taken an elephant.

The merchant dismounted and walked across to dry land. He sat down where he had sat for so long previously, and looked directly into the stricken donkey's eyes.

"Now, my friend, what is it to be? Will we work together again, or will you continue to work against me?"

These words were beyond the donkey's comprehension, but it well understood its lesson.

Dr Ken Spillman is the author of more than 50 books including the internationally popular Jake series. Based in Australia, Ken travels frequently and has spoken to more than 70,000 children in the past four years. He is a long-time advocate for writers and writing in the Asian region and actively supports organisations connecting marginalised children with the world of stories. For more information, visit: www.kenspillman.com.

Suvidha Mistry is a freelance illustrator with a passion for all forms of art. She loves to tell stories with her illustrations, sketches and photographs. She has worked with multimedia firms as a graphic head and is now living her dream of being an illustrator of children's books.

Other Books by Ken Spillman

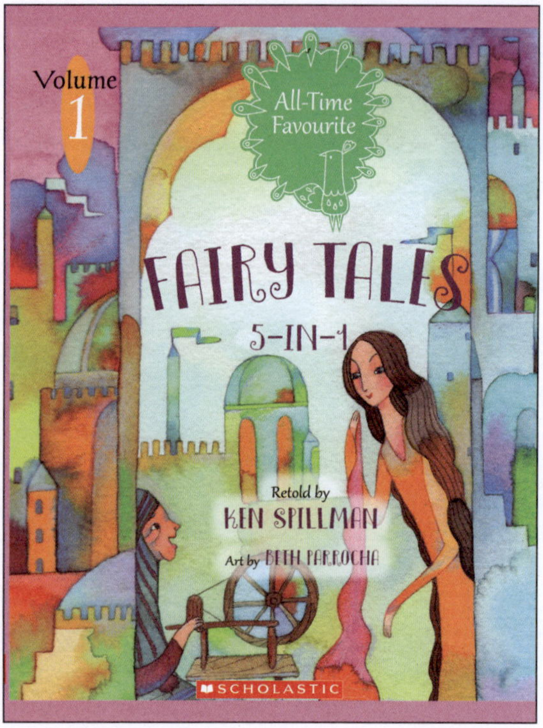

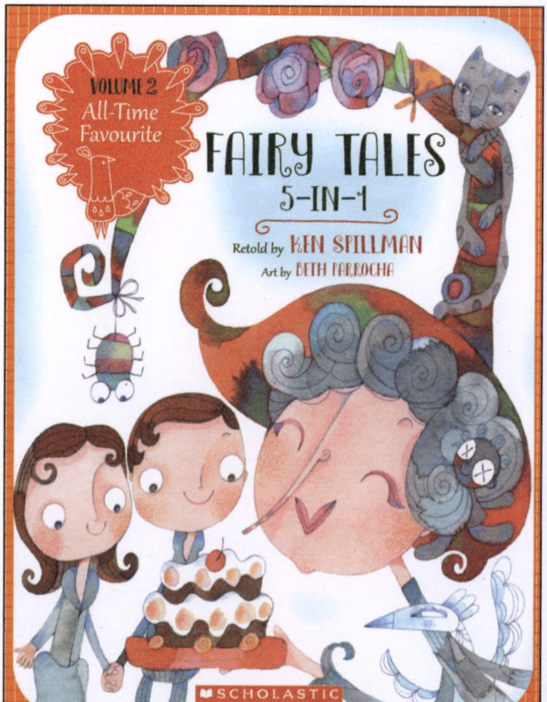